Did Fleming
RESCUE
Churchill?

A Research Puzzle

James Cross Giblin

Did Fleming
RESCUE
Churchill?

A Research Puzzle

SIR
ALEXANDER
FLEMING
BY
JASON

Illustrated by Erik Brooks

Henry Holt and Company
New York

Henry Holt and Company, LLC
Publishers since 1866
175 Fifth Avenue
New York, New York 10010
www.HenryHoltKids.com

Library of Congress Cataloging-in-Publication Data
Giblin, James.
Did Fleming rescue Churchill? : a research puzzle / by James Cross Giblin ;
illustrated by Erik Brooks.—1st ed.
p.   cm.
Summary: Ten-year-old Jason uses everything he knows about research, including
how to separate fact from fiction when using the Internet, to make the deadline
for his history paper on scientist Alexander Fleming—the discoverer of penicillin.
Includes research tips, emphasizing the importance of accuracy.
Includes bibliographical references (p.   ).
ISBN-13: 978-0-8050-8183-1 / ISBN-10: 0-8050-8183-6
[1. Research—Fiction. 2. Homework—Fiction. 3. Schools—Fiction.
4. Fleming, Alexander, 1881–1955—Fiction.] I. Brooks, Erik, ill. II. Title.
PZ7.G3392533Di 2008
[Fic]—dc22
2007027568

First Edition—2008
Printed in the United States of America on acid-free paper. ∞

1 3 5 7 9 10 8 6 4 2

For Nina Ignatowicz
—J. C. G.

For Mrs. Apodaca
—E. B.

Contents

CHAPTER ONE

A Terrific Story

On Tuesday, I woke up with a bad toothache, and that's how I got stuck with Sir Alexander Fleming. It happened this way. Mom made an emergency appointment with the dentist for that afternoon, which meant I had to miss Social Studies. And during Social Studies, Ms. O'Mara assigned the subjects for the three-page biographies of famous scientists that we have to write by next Monday.

The really interesting scientists got taken right away—people like the Wright brothers and Thomas Edison and that German guy, Wernher von Braun, who designed rockets for the Nazis and then for the United States. By the time I went back to school on Wednesday, the only scientist left on Ms. O'Mara's list was someone I'd never heard of: Sir Alexander Fleming.

I went up to the teacher's desk after class. "Isn't there anybody else I can write about?" I asked.

But Ms. O'Mara wouldn't budge. "Jason," she said, "Alexander Fleming made a great contribution to humanity. He discovered penicillin, the antibiotic that has saved millions of lives. I'm sure you can find lots of fascinating things to write about him."

"Okay," I said grudgingly. "I'll look him up on the Internet when I get home."

"I wouldn't start with the Internet," Ms. O'Mara said.

"Why not?"

"Because a lot of stuff on it isn't accurate, Jason, and it's hard to tell what is and what isn't. I'd begin instead by reading a book or an encyclopedia article to get the basic facts about Fleming. Then you can go on the Internet for more information."

"Okay," I said, but I wasn't happy. First I get an assignment to write about this Fleming guy, and then I had to start by reading some boring book or article. At least my tooth didn't hurt anymore. Whatever Dr. Di Prima had done had solved *that* problem.

At dinner, I told Dad and Mom about my assignment, but they weren't much help. "Who was Alexander Fleming?" Dad asked absentmindedly, and Mom said, "Wasn't he the man who discovered the vaccine for polio?"

"No, Mom. He discovered penicillin," I said. "But that's all I know about him."

Grandma—Mom's mom—had come over for dinner that evening. She wasn't helpful either. In fact, she made me feel worse when she said, "I'm surprised you have to write reports, with source notes and everything, when you're in fifth grade. We didn't have to do anything like that until we were in high school."

The next day, Thursday, I got excused from study hall to go to the library. I found two biographies of Fleming, but they were both long and had almost no pictures. And when I read the first couple of pages, they both sounded dull.

Maybe I'd have better luck with the encyclopedias. There was a short article about Fleming in the first one. It said that he was born in 1881 and

died in 1955, and a little bit about how he discovered penicillin. But there was no way I could stretch out the information to fill three pages.

The next encyclopedia looked more promising. It was all about science and scientists, and had a much longer article about Fleming. I decided I'd better read the whole article and make notes, but I felt discouraged when I finished. Fleming's big discovery came about by accident, the article said. And he didn't really follow through on it. Two other scientists picked up where Fleming left off, tested penicillin, and proved that it worked. How could I make an interesting biography out of that?

On Friday, I began to get really worried. The report was due on Monday, and I still didn't know much of anything about Alexander Fleming. After Social Studies class, I went up to Ms. O'Mara's desk again. I thought I heard her sigh when she saw me coming.

"Yes, Jason, what is it?" she asked as she put some papers in her briefcase.

"I went to the library like you said, and read a couple of encyclopedia articles about Alexander Fleming, but they didn't tell me a whole lot. He discovered penicillin, but then he sort of stopped. Two other guys took it from there." I raised my voice a little to get her attention. "I don't know where to go next, Ms. O'Mara, and Monday is just a couple of days away. Do you have any suggestions?"

The louder voice seemed to work. Ms. O'Mara turned to me and focused on my problem. "Maybe it's time for you to go on the Internet," she said. "You could look up the other two scientists who worked on penicillin, and see if there are some interesting facts about them. Or you could search for information about penicillin itself—how it works and why it's successful in fighting infections."

She sounded more and more enthusiastic as

she went on: "Or you could try to find some colorful anecdotes about Alexander Fleming that would help to bring him to life—"

"Excuse me, Ms. O'Mara," I interrupted. "What's an anecdote?"

"A funny or dramatic true story about something."

"How can I find one?"

"I'd start with a search for 'anecdotes about Alexander Fleming' or 'stories about Alexander Fleming' and see if that turns up anything. But, remember, they can't just be good stories. They have to be something that really happened."

She got me fired up about the idea, and I turned on my computer as soon as I got home. I went to a search engine, typed in "stories about Alexander Fleming" like Ms. O'Mara suggested, and right away a bunch of possibilities appeared on the screen. Maybe I was having some good luck for a change! I clicked on the first item on the list, and this is what came up:

His name was Fleming, and he was a poor Scottish farmer. One day, while plowing a rocky field, he heard a cry for help coming from a nearby bog. He dropped his tools and ran to the bog. There, mired to his neck in thick black mud, was a terrified boy, screaming and struggling to free himself. Farmer Fleming waded into the mud, reached out to the boy, and pulled him out of the bog. He saved the lad from what could have been a slow and terrifying

death. The boy thanked Farmer Fleming and, after catching his breath, ran down the road toward his home. The next day, a fancy carriage pulled up in front of Farmer Fleming's humble cottage. An elegantly dressed nobleman stepped out and introduced himself as the father of the boy Farmer Fleming had rescued.

"I want to repay you," the nobleman said. "You saved my son's life."

"Any caring person would have done what I did," Farmer Fleming replied. "I can't accept payment for it." At that moment, the farmer's son came to the door of the cottage.

"Is that your son?" the nobleman asked.

"Yes," the farmer replied proudly.

"I'll make you a deal," the nobleman said. "Let me provide your boy with the same level of education my own son will enjoy. If the lad is anything like his father, he'll grow up to be a man we both will be proud of."

And that the boy did. Young Fleming attended the very best schools and, in time, graduated from St. Mary's Hospital Medical School in London. He went on to become known throughout the world as the noted Sir Alexander Fleming, the discoverer of penicillin.

Years afterward, the same nobleman's son who was saved from the bog was stricken with pneumonia. What saved his life this time? Penicillin. What was the name of the nobleman? Lord Randolph Churchill. And what was his son's name? Sir Winston Churchill, the prime minister who led Great Britain to victory in World War II. As someone once said, "What goes around comes around."

When I finished reading the story, I let out a yell. This was *just* what I needed to make Fleming's biography interesting. But then I noticed a note in smaller type at the bottom of the screen.

This is a wonderful story, isn't it? The poor Scottish farmer saving the young Winston Churchill's life; Churchill's father, in his gratitude, vowing to pay for the education of the farmer's son; and the son growing up to discover penicillin, which in turn saves the adult Winston's life. The only problem with the tale is that it probably isn't true.

Not true? Oh, no! I dig up this terrific story, but then I find out it probably isn't true. And Ms. O'Mara said that any story I include in Fleming's biography *had* to be true.

Wait a minute, though. Those last sentences didn't say the story *definitely* wasn't true, only that it *probably* wasn't. Eagerly, I switched back to the complete list of stories about Alexander Fleming. Maybe some of the other listings told the same story, and maybe they contained proof that it was true.

CHAPTER TWO

But Is It True?

I was just about to click on the second listing when Mom called me to come to dinner. And she didn't sound like she'd listen to any excuses. I put the computer on "sleep" and hurried downstairs.

Dad noticed that I was eating more quickly than usual. "What's the rush?" he asked.

"I want to get back online," I said. "I'm doing research for that report I told you about, and I think I'm on to something."

"I can't remember when I've seen you so eager to do homework," Mom said.

"This is different," I replied. "It isn't just homework—it's research!"

Suddenly I remembered something Ms. O'Mara had said when she told us about the assignment. "Research can really be fun when you get into it. It's a lot like playing detective." At the time I thought she was just giving us a pep talk, but now I knew what she meant.

Upstairs I discovered that the second story was almost exactly the same as the first one. The only difference was that this time it was Alexander, not his father, who pulled young Winston Churchill out of the bog.

Like in the other story, Lord Randolph Churchill wanted to pay Alexander for saving

his son, but Alexander refused. Then Lord Randolph asked him what he wanted to be when he grew up, and Alexander said, "A doctor." But he was sure it would never happen because his father couldn't afford to send him to medical school.

Lord Randolph said that was no problem, and he offered to pay for Alexander's education. Alexander got to go to medical school, and a few years after he graduated, he discovered penicillin. The story ended just like the first one did, when the grown-up Winston Churchill got sick with pneumonia and Alexander's discovery helped to save his life.

When I finished reading, I didn't know what to think. It was strange that Alexander's father saved Winston in the first story, while Alexander saved him in the second. But whoever wrote down the stories may just have gotten mixed up about that. I was feeling hopeful as I scrolled farther down and saw that there was a note after the end of this story, too. Maybe it would clear everything up.

It did—but not the way I wanted. The note said, "Although this is an appealing story, it is apparently a myth. An inheritance from an uncle, not a gift from Lord Randolph Churchill, enabled Alexander to enroll in medical school. Biographies of Alexander Fleming and Winston Churchill make no mention of them ever meeting. Churchill did get pneumonia in 1945, but there is no evidence he was treated with penicillin."

That sounded pretty definite. But I wasn't ready to give up yet. Maybe the other writers had it wrong about where Alexander got the money to go to medical school. And about Alexander and Churchill never meeting. There were a couple more items on the list. I decided to check them out and clicked on the first one. It turned out to be the same story—but different from either of the others.

In this story, Winston's father, Lord Randolph Churchill, was the one who got into trouble. He was vacationing in Scotland when his carriage got stuck in the mud along a country road. Luckily, young Alexander came along just then, leading a pair of strong draft horses. He hitched them alongside Churchill's horses, and together they pulled Lord Randolph's carriage out of the mud.

From there on, the story was just like the others. Lord Randolph paid for Alexander's medical school education, Alexander discovered penicillin, and years later the medicine saved Winston Churchill's life.

By now I was having a hard time believing the story. There was just too much about it that seemed made up. But there was one more item on the search list, a link to a site called the Churchill Centre. I figured it must be an English site since they didn't spell *center* the way we do.

I clicked on the site, and a menu came up on the screen. One of the items on it was "Churchill Facts." Maybe I'd find the story there, and if I did, it might tell me once and for all whether it was true or false. I clicked again.

Up came a list of frequently asked questions about Churchill, and would you believe it? The very first one was "Did Sir Alexander Fleming save Winston Churchill's life?" I scrolled down quickly for the answer.

> The story that Sir Alexander Fleming or his father (the renditions vary) saved Churchill's life has been roaring around the Internet lately. We must have had fifty e-mails about it.

That sounded promising, but then came the kicker.

> Charming as the story is, it is certainly fiction. It apparently originated in *Worship Programs for Juniors,* by Alice A. Bays and Elizabeth Jones Oakbery, published around 1950 by an American religious publisher. The story appeared in a chapter entitled "The Power of Kindness."

Well, now I knew—and I wished I didn't. The story that was going to be the high point of my biography of Fleming—and take up at least three-quarters of a page—wasn't true. There was no way I could use it. I put the computer to sleep and leaned back in my chair.

Here I was on Friday night with the report due on Monday. And a lot of the material I was going to put in it had just vanished into thin air—poof! Where could I possibly find something to fill in for the story of Alexander and Winston?

Suddenly I had an idea. Maybe there *was* a way I could use the story after all, even if it wasn't true! I glanced at my watch. It was too late to start writing now. I'd have to wait until tomorrow morning.

CHAPTER THREE

"Wake Up, Jason!"

On Saturday, right after breakfast, I gathered together my research—the copies I'd made of the encyclopedia articles about Fleming and the printouts of the different stories about how he saved Winston Churchill. Then I turned on the computer, clicked "blank," and began to write.

I didn't have too much time because Mom was going to drive me to the mall around eleven to meet my friend Dominic and see a new action movie with lots of great special effects. Any other Saturday, I'd be looking forward to the movie, but today—with the deadline for the report hanging over me like a storm cloud—I almost wished I wasn't going.

When I got home from the movie, I hurried upstairs and picked up where I'd left off. I was almost through with the part about Fleming's life by dinnertime. But that was only the first half. I still had to figure out how to work in the three stories.

After dinner, I was too tired to do anything but watch TV. I had a hard time concentrating on the program though. I kept thinking about the report and wondering when I was ever going to have time to finish it. Sunday morning I'd be going to church with Mom and Dad, and Sunday afternoon we were invited to a barbecue at Uncle Mike and Aunt Ellen's house.

There was only one way out. Much as I'd hate to miss Uncle Mike's grilled burgers and Aunt Ellen's deviled eggs, I'd have to skip the barbecue.

I felt really bad about that. But writing a good report had become the most important thing in my life right then. I wasn't sure exactly why; I just knew I wanted to give it my best shot, as Dad often says. Working hard and fast, I finished the report and the list of my sources just before he and Mom came home on Sunday evening.

On Monday, I got up early to read over the report, make a few final changes, and do a spell-check. Then I printed out two copies—one for Ms. O'Mara, the other for me. It ended up filling four pages. Ms. O'Mara might not like anything else about the report, but at least she couldn't say it was too short!

I put the report in my backpack and raced to

the corner where the school bus stopped. Today of all days I didn't want to miss it. My morning classes dragged by, but at last it was time for Social Studies. After waiting eagerly all day for this class, I entered the room slowly. Now that the moment had finally arrived, I was hesitant about turning in my report. The idea I'd had for it seemed like a good one while I was writing, but I wasn't so sure anymore. Would Ms. O'Mara go along with it? Or would she think I'd just taken an easy way out?

Ms. O'Mara asked us to pass our reports to the front of the class, and I added mine to the stack. I was glad to see the last of it—at least for a while. But then Ms. O'Mara promised to read the reports right away and have them ready to give back to us by Friday. Why did it have to be so soon?

On Friday, I was prepared for the worst. It didn't help matters that the cafeteria had my least favorite dish for lunch: Tuna Surprise—a big glob of tuna salad on a single piece of melba toast, surrounded by a circle of tasteless pink tomato wedges. I guess it was supposed to be healthy.

After lunch, I sat back in my seat in Social Studies and told myself I didn't care what happened. By then I'd managed to convince myself that Ms. O'Mara must hate what I'd done. My only hope was that she'd give the report at least a passing grade so I wouldn't have to answer a lot of questions from my parents.

Ms. O'Mara began by telling everyone how good the reports were. Except for mine, I thought. I was so deep in gloom that I didn't realize she'd changed the subject until Adam Stern nudged my arm. (Adam sits across from me.)

"Wake up, Jason," he said. "Ms. O'Mara is talking about you!"

CHAPTER FOUR

Rotten Melons Save Lives

I sat up in my seat to face the teacher and couldn't believe what I heard next. "Jason's biography deserves special praise," she said, "because of the way he solved a difficult problem."

So she liked what I'd done! All my doubts and worries suddenly seemed silly. But then

Ms. O'Mara had to go and spoil my happy mood.

"I'll read Jason's report now so you can see what I mean," she said.

I could feel everyone's eyes on me and wished I could shrink down to nothing. Why did she have to read my report out loud? The kids might laugh in all the wrong places. Or else they might sigh and groan with boredom. I didn't know which would be worse.

Ms. O'Mara picked up the report and began to read. "I didn't want to write about Sir Alexander Fleming—I didn't even know who he was," she said. Someone in back of me giggled, but Ms. O'Mara went on. "I didn't have any choice, though. All the interesting scientists had been taken by the time I got my assignment."

Everyone seemed to be listening, so I relaxed a little as Ms. O'Mara continued to read.

In an encyclopedia I found out that Alexander Fleming was born in Scotland on August 6, 1881. His father was a farmer, and Alexander had seven brothers and sisters. Alexander was next to the youngest. When he was fourteen, his father died, and Alexander wondered what would become of him—and his family.

One of his older brothers, Tom, was a doctor in London. Alexander and his two other brothers and a sister went to live with Tom. In London, Alexander studied at the Polytechnic School, which was sort of like a high school. When he graduated, he got a job as a clerk in a shipping office, and he worked there for four years, but he didn't like it.

Tom suggested he study medicine, so Alexander went to St. Mary's Medical School at the University of London. He graduated from St. Mary's in 1906, and stayed on at the school to do research in bacteriology. (That's the study of one-celled creatures, some of which cause diseases.) Then World War I started in 1914.

The class was still paying attention, and I relaxed even more. Ms. O'Mara's voice got really dramatic in the next part, the one about the war.

> *Alexander joined the British army as a captain in the Army Medical Corps. He helped to set up a battlefield hospital just behind the front lines in France.*
>
> *Most of the fighting in World War I was done from trenches, which were like deep ditches. The British and French armies would be in one trench, and the German army would be in another trench. The trenches were just a few yards apart. In a battle, one army would try to climb out of its trench and move forward, but it would get pushed back. Then the other army would try to climb out of its trench, and it would get pushed back. Bullets flew everywhere, and many soldiers were killed or wounded.*
>
> *Alexander and the other doctors had a*

hard time treating the wounded. They had no powerful antibiotics—those are substances that can fight the bacteria that cause disease. Injured soldiers were brought by the dozens to Alexander's hospital. They would be in terrible pain from gaping wounds. But Alexander couldn't help them because he didn't have the medicines they needed. Instead he *would just have to stand and watch as the wounds got infected. The infections spread, and most of the soldiers died horrible deaths.*

By then everyone was listening hard to Ms. O'Mara, even kids like Buddy Jensen and Kurt Kapszinski, who never listened to anybody.

After the war ended, Alexander couldn't forget all those wounded soldiers on the battlefield. He decided he would try to find an antibiotic that would cure terrible infections like theirs. A few years later he discovered lysozyme, which is found in many body fluids like saliva and tears. He tested it and found that it worked against some infections. But it didn't work against the strongest ones.

He kept searching, and in 1928 he made an important discovery by accident. He had been growing a bunch of bacteria for his studies in a petri dish.

One day he was examining the bacteria
and he left the lid off the dish a little too
long. A mold spore got into the dish and
landed on the bacteria and began to grow.
But Alexander didn't see it because he'd
gone on vacation.

As Ms. O'Mara read on, I got caught up in my own writing. But then a couple of kids in back of me groaned. I hoped it was because they were caught up in the story, too.

Ms. O'Mara ignored the groans and continued to read.

When Alexander got back, he looked at the petri dish and was very surprised. The mold had kept on growing, and he noticed something even more puzzling. Wherever the mold had grown, the bacteria had disappeared. Alexander guessed that the mold contained something that killed the bacteria.

Ms. O'Mara paused for a moment before continuing.

Alexander examined the mold and identified it as Penicillium notatum *(that's its name in Latin). Then he separated out the material that was killing the bacteria and named it penicillin. He made many tests with penicillin and different kinds of bacteria, and discovered you couldn't always count on the penicillin to work. Sometimes it killed the harmful bacteria, and sometimes it didn't.*

In 1929, Alexander wrote up the results of his tests for a science magazine. He said that penicillin might be a valuable antibiotic in treating infections. But that would only happen if it could be made to work all the time and not just sometimes. And once that had been done, there would be another problem: A way would have to be found to produce lots of penicillin to meet the demand from doctors everywhere.

Ms. O'Mara paused again and looked around the class.

Having gotten this far, you'd think Alexander would have kept right on going.

But he didn't. He published one more article about penicillin in 1931, and then he stopped his research and went on to other things.

It wasn't until 1938 that two other scientists working in Britain, Dr. Howard Florey and Dr. Ernst Chain, picked up where Alexander left off. After reading Fleming's articles, they gave shots of penicillin to live mice that were suffering from bacterial infections. The mice were cured. Then Dr. Florey and Dr. Chain gave shots of the antibiotic to some human volunteers with similar infections. Penicillin cured their infections, too.

By then it was 1940, and England was at war with Nazi Germany. Like in the First World War, there was a big demand for antibiotics to treat the soldiers' wounds. Dr. Florey and Dr. Chain helped find ways to produce more penicillin for the army doctors. But I don't think Alexander played any part in that.

In 1944, the king of England, George VI, knighted Alexander for his contributions to science. Now he was known as Sir Alexander Fleming. The king knighted Dr. Florey, too, but not Dr. Chain. Then, in 1945, Alexander received the Nobel Prize for medicine. This time, though, the judges realized how much Dr. Chain had contributed to the development of penicillin, and both he and Dr. Florey shared the Nobel Prize with Alexander.

Sir Alexander Fleming died on March 11, 1955. He was buried in St. Paul's Cathedral in London. That's where lots of kings and queens and other famous English people are buried. But when I got to the end of Alexander's biography, I was disappointed. His big discovery was an accident, and he didn't do anything much to follow through on it. I didn't see how I could write more than a page or maybe a page and a half about his life. And the report had to be at least three pages.

Someone laughed, and someone else said, "I had the same problem."

Ms. O'Mara said, "I think a lot of you probably did. But let's see how Jason solved his. That's where his report gets really interesting." She began to read again.

I told Ms. O'Mara about the trouble I was having, and she suggested I try to find an anecdote about something interesting that Alexander did. But she said it couldn't be just a good story. It had to be true. So I went on the Internet and found a great story about Alexander right away.

Then Ms. O'Mara read the story of how Alexander's father saved Winston Churchill's life, and how Churchill's father offered to pay for Alexander's education as a reward.

Next, she read the other two stories I'd discovered—the one where Alexander himself saved

Winston, and the one where Alexander helped to pull Winston's father's carriage out of the mud.

Finally, she read about the last article I found on the Internet, the one that said there was no way any of the stories could possibly have happened.

She paused. "What do you think Jason did then? Remember, I told him any anecdote—any story—he used in his report had to be true."

"He tried to pretend it *was* true," someone said.

"But you caught him!" someone else chimed in.

"No, neither of those," Ms. O'Mara said. "Here's what he did do." And she began to read again.

When I got to the end of the article about the story, my heart sank. I was counting on the story to fill out Alexander's biography and make it more interesting. But it wasn't true. Then I had a thought. When you're writing a biography, you can't believe something is true just because someone says it is. You have to check it out, the way I checked out the story about how Alexander saved Winston.

That doesn't mean you can't include it though. You just have to say, as I'm saying now, that it's a good story that unfortunately didn't happen. And including it proves one thing—that I really did my research.

Laughter rippled around the room.

Ms. O'Mara waited for it to die down before she went on.

But I didn't want to end Alexander's biography there. Instead, I wanted to end it with an anecdote that really did happen. I mentioned before that Dr. Florey and Dr. Chain helped to fill the demand for lots of penicillin during World War II. Here's how they did it. The two doctors had discovered that the penicillin mold grew especially well on corn. But farmers didn't raise much corn in England. It was a more important crop in the United States.

So Dr. Florey came to America, and he ended up in Illinois. Farmers grew a lot of corn in Illinois. Dr. Florey worked with American scientists, and together they discovered that Illinois corn produced five hundred times as much penicillin mold as anything had before.

But Dr. Florey and the scientists didn't stop there. They searched for other sources and found one in a strange place. A market in Peoria, Illinois, was about to throw out some rotting cantaloupe melons.

Dr. Florey offered to take the melons away, and guess what? When spores of the Penicillium mold got on the melons,

they went crazy. As flies buzzed around,
the mold grew and grew and grew! The
stink was awful, but nothing had ever
produced as much penicillin as those
rotten melons.

"Yuck!" shouted Kurt Kapszinski.

"Really gross!" someone added.

"Did the penicillin smell bad, too?" someone else asked.

Ms. O'Mara smiled at me as she folded the pages of my report and put them down. I thought I even saw her wink.

I couldn't have been happier with everyone's reactions. "Thanks, Alexander," I said silently. "You turned out to be a good subject for a biography after all."

Tips on Doing Research

1. In the story Jason had to write a biographical report on Sir Alexander Fleming. But when you're assigned to write a report, you can often choose the topic. If so, be sure to pick one that interests you. Maybe the zoo in a nearby city is one of your favorite places, so you decide to write about it.

2. Before you start the research, you'll need to know what you want to cover in your report. Possible topics might include:
    (a) The history of the zoo. When was it founded? How big is it?
    (b) The animals and birds that live in the zoo. How many are there? Do they live in cages or in areas that resemble their natural homes? Do the animals come from all over the world? What are some of the most popular ones?

3. Once you know what you'll be writing about, think about where and how you can find the facts you'll need.
    (a) If you want to begin with some material about zoos in general, then go to the library and look for books and encyclopedia articles about zoos.

(b) On the other hand, if you choose to focus on your local zoo, start by entering the zoo's name on a computer search engine. Once you have the zoo's Web address, you can check to see what's on its menu. Items labeled History, Description, and Animals are likely to have the answers you need.

(c) Print out the information so that you can refer to it when you're ready to start writing. (And so that you'll have it on hand when you compile the list of sources your teacher will probably want you to turn in with the report.)

4. Illustrations will make your report more lively and colorful. Check to see if the zoo's Web site contains photos of the zoo grounds and the animals that live on them. Download the pictures and print out those you think are the most interesting. (If you were writing an article for publication, you'd have to get permission from the zoo to use its pictures and probably pay a fee for them. But zoos and other institutions usually don't charge for pictures used in school assignments.)

5. Nothing is more helpful when doing research than visiting the place you're writing about. If the zoo is close enough, maybe you can get someone to take

you there. You can make notes or take pictures of what you see. You may also find brochures about some of the exhibits—the monkey island, the pool where seals swim, the aviary where eagles soar. These brochures are likely to contain information you won't find on the Internet.

6. On your visit, keep your eye out for primary source material. These are writings or recordings people have made of things they've experienced firsthand. Maybe a zookeeper has described what it's like to feed the seals, or a zoo dentist has told how he takes care of an elephant's teeth. Material such as this will help bring the zoo to life for your readers. Chances are you'll find the material in the information center, if the zoo has one, or in the bookstore or gift shop.

7. Gather more research material than you'll need. Then you can pick and choose and include only the most interesting and unusual facts in your report. Just be sure, like Jason, to check and double-check each fact that you do include. This will ensure that everything in your report is accurate. And accuracy is the goal of every nonfiction writer, young and old.

Sources

When I was preparing to write this story, I researched the same sources—an encyclopedia and the Internet—that Jason might have used. All the facts about Alexander Fleming and the discovery of penicillin are correct, and the three variations on the tale of Winston's rescue conform to those Jason might have discovered on the Internet. However, I trimmed and reworded the variations to avoid repetition and to highlight the elements a bright ten-year-old might have found especially interesting.

The main topics in the story, and the sources for each, are listed below in the order in which they appear in the narrative.

The Tale

1. The first version of the story, "What Goes Around," in which Farmer Fleming saves young Winston Churchill's life, and the second version, in which Alexander Fleming himself rescues Winston Churchill:

    Urban Legends Reference Pages. *Alexander Fleming's Father and Winston Churchill.* [Updated 22 February 2007; cited 28 February

2007.] Available from www.snopes.com/glurge/fleming.htm.

2. The third version, in which Alexander Fleming rescues Lord Randolph Churchill:

    The School for Champions: online lessons for those seeking success. *Winston Churchill: The Early and Journalist Years*. [Updated 6 February 2006; cited 28 February 2007.] Available from www.school-for-champions.com/biographies/churchill.htm.

3. The explanation of why the tale is not true:

    Sir Winston Churchill: The Churchill Centre. *FAQs: Personal: Did Sir Alexander Fleming Save Churchill's Life?* [Cited 28 February 2007.] Available from http://www.winstonchurchill.org/i4a/pages/index.cfm?pageid=433.

Sir Alexander Fleming

1. *Columbia Encyclopedia*, fifth edition. Boston: Houghton Mifflin Company, 1993.

2. Nobelprize.org. *Sir Alexander Fleming Biography*. [Cited 28 February 2007.] Available from http://nobelprize.org/nobel_prizes/medicine/laureates/1945/fleming-bio.html. [Originally from *Nobel Lectures, Physiology or*

Medicine, 1942–1962, Amsterdam: Elsevier Publishing Company, 1964.]

3. Britannia: British History. *Biographies of Great Men and Women of England, Wales, and Scotland.* [Cited 28 February 2007.] Available from http://www.britannia.com/bios/fleming.html.

4. PBS. *A Science Odyssey: People and Discoveries: Alexander Fleming.* [Cited 28 February 2007.] Available from http://www.pbs.org/wgbh/aso/databank/entries/bmflem.html. (Includes links to information on Howard Florey and the anecdote about rotting melons as a good source of penicillin.)

Dr. Ernst Chain

PBS. *A Science Odyssey: People and Discoveries: Ernst Chain.* [Cited 28 February 2007.] Available from http://www.pbs.org/wgbh/aso/databank/entries/bmchai.html.

Penicillin

1. *Columbia Encyclopedia*, fifth edition. Boston: Houghton Mifflin Company, 1993.
2. KU Information Technology. *Jack's Bugs in the News*, What the Heck Is Penicillin? [Cited 28 February 2007.] Available from www.people.ku.edu/~jbrown/penicillin.html.